This book is dedicated in loving memory of Charles B. Wagner.

CONTENTS

Dedication

Untimely Delivery   1

Tea at Tiffany's   14

The Sabinarath of Xenoscythe   21

The Trial of Tokarov   33

UNTIMELY DELIVERY

By Kevin Marlow

Jennette popped awake, rolling her head to look at the alarm clock, it was 4:39 am, almost an hour before the alarm was set to wake. A feeling of discomfort brewed in her gut. Thirty seconds later her insides felt like a pile of snakes writhing on hot coals. Putting a hand over her mouth, she bounced out of bed and ran for the bathroom. Sliding on her knees, she flipped up the seat on the toilet. The puke splattered into the bowl, the taste of bile forcing a couple more dry heaves.

Standing up Jennette twisted the wobbly chrome handle on the vanity faucet and filled the flimsy plastic cup used to rinse her mouth after brushing her teeth. Swishing and spitting, she tried to get the vomit taste out of her mouth. Splashing water on her face, she rubbed the crust from her eyelids and pulled the towel from the rack to dry herself.

Looking in the mirror, framed by a slightly rusted medicine cabinet, she paused. *God, I look old.* Crows feet were creeping from the hairline to the edge of sky-blue eyes. Wisps of gray were sprinkled in dishwater blonde hair. Craning her head up, the skin on her neck was starting to sag and wrinkle. She smiled at the reflection. Not sure if she was actually happy, it felt forced, like she was trying to will herself to be happy.

Sliding open the cabinet she grabbed a bottle of multicolored wafers and tapped a few into her palm and tossed them in her mouth. Crunching them as she tousled her hair, she inched in close to the mirror. *My pores look like craters!* Aging was freaking her out. It felt like the four years she spent in prison had made her ten years older.

After a shower, she dressed in her freshly washed uniform and pinned a name tag on the front of her blouse. It was a morning shift on a Monday. Lou's Diner would be full of blue collars needing to fuel up before doing the digging, sawing, and pounding that kept their sleepy Midwest town humming along.

A dented blue Chevy creaked when she pulled open the door. The worn key felt loose in the ignition. If she didn't wiggle the gearshift a little it wouldn't turn over. The four cylinder grumbled to life and pulled her to work.

"You have the four tops over by the door." Lou was the owner/manager/cook. "Natalie has the bar and other tables."

Jennette forced a grin at Lou and started wiping down the tables. Her stomach wasn't done aggravating. An hour into the shift she excused herself, pulled off her apron, and hurried to the bathroom. After retching in the stall for a bit, she tried to clean up in the tiny sink.

"Sorry Lou, my belly has been bugging me all morning." Lou gave her the 'toughen up' look as he slid a full breakfast plate with a side of pancakes towards her.

The morning shift stretched until 3 pm, by then her nausea had subsided. Pulling tips from the apron she counted 67 dollars and 13 cents. She waved to Lou and Natalie and headed for the glass exit door. Looking up she saw the Norman Rockwell calendar on the wall and noticed the day. It was July 11. *Oh shit! My last period was six weeks ago.*

Later that night, she kept her eyes closed and her hand tingled with nerves holding the plastic wand. Opening them, there it was, two blue lines. *I'm pregnant.*

"Breaking news, the supreme court has reversed Roe vs. Wade. Any states with trigger laws on abortion have outlawed the procedure effective immediately." The newscaster droned on from the television in the background. Jennette lived in a deep red state, one where people spray painted 'God, Guns and Guts' on the tailgates of their rusty pickups. *What are the chances of ending up preggers the day your state outlawed abortion?* She needed to call her mom.

"I don't know what to do Mom. I'm pregnant."

"What?!? Oh Jen, don't tell me that. How?"

"I don't know. Well, I know how, I just can't believe it. I always take precautions."

"Aren't you on the pill?"

"No, I can't afford it. I can barely make rent Mom."

"Well, I can't help you, Jen. Since I moved into assisted housing there isn't much left over after I pay my bills."

"What about Uncle Rob and Auntie Faye?"

"What are you gonna do, ask them for money?"

"I can get an abortion in Illinois. I'll tell them it is for a car repair or something." Her aunt and uncle were deeply religious and regulars at church. Jen's mom always said they were rich. Jennette felt the tug of her old ways, 'A bitch has to do what she can to get by,' was one of her sayings from back in the day.

"I don't know hun. If they ask me, I'll have to lie about it." Her mom was getting distraught. "I'll talk to you later."

Jennette stared at the motel wall, finally able to hold down a job, her paycheck put a roof over her head. Her car ran well enough to keep her from having to walk to work, and now this. She couldn't tell what's his name, he was sleeping on his brother-in-law's back porch on a couch, still begging her for cigarette money after they had sex.

Having stayed clean for her first six months of parole, a shiver shot through her body. She looked down at her arm. The thought of puncturing herself with a needle made her smile. Her body ached to feel the ice water coursing through her veins, and the blissful moment when one started to nod as the opioids massaged the pleasure centers in the brain. *What the hell am I thinking?*

Four years in prison for dealing dope hadn't erased the yearning for a high. Like an invisible demon, it lurked just out of sight, waiting for moments of weakness to remind you how it would all disappear, if only for a while if you just gave in to the urge.

Jennette pulled a frozen dinner from the tiny fridge and slapped it in the microwave. As she chewed on the rubbery breaded chicken, she tried to imagine what she could say to her Aunt and Uncle. 'My car broke down and I can't get to work. I'm behind on my rent and I'm going to be homeless. I only need 500.00 dollars this time, I promise I'll pay you back when I can.'

They had heard it before. Before she was incarcerated she had made up every lie imaginable to keep dope in her needle. They cut her off when she was arrested for dealing heroin. The words stung, 'I can't believe you're a junkie.' Faye's face loomed in her mind, wiping at tears with a tissue seated behind her in the courtroom. She remembered looking at her family as the officer led her out of the room in handcuffs and felt nothing. After a year in lockup, a counselor said something that broke through her selfish façade. 'You're not just hurting yourself, you're hurting the ones you love.'

Laying on the bed, staring at the flatscreen watching the news, her old and new self wrestled for control. She couldn't be a mother. She could barely take care of herself. Picturing herself bloated and waddling around waiting tables at the restaurant, she cringed. *I can't even afford to take a day off work.*

Sleep was fitful that night, hot flashes came, forcing her to throw off the covers. At 3 am Jennette retrieved the quart tub of store-brand chocolate ice cream from the cramped freezer and sat in the dark, eating spoon after spoon, till she was scraping the waxy paper at the bottom of the tub and sucking on the spoon.

The next day work flew by, she planned on driving over past the next town to her Aunt and Uncle's house after her shift. It would be better to ask in person. They hadn't talked in a few months. The summer sun scorched the blacktop road. The rains of June had dried up leaving the woods and fields cracked and broken. She pushed the dial on the FM radio. 'Papa Don't Preach' by Madonna crackled over the car stereo. Tapping on the steering wheel, she suddenly noticed the vivid green of the leaves on the trees as they swayed in the hot summer wind.

Humming along, Jen sang the chorus, "Papa

don't preach, I'm in trouble deep, Papa don't preach, I've been losing sleep, But I made up my mind, I'm keeping my baby." Realizing what she just sang, she pushed the button and turned it off. *That was weird.*

Corn fields whizzed by, anchored above by puffy white clouds and brilliant blue skies. Old barns hinted at simpler times when everyone around tried to farm their way out of poverty. Uncle Rob sold most of the farm years ago. They kept the house and a few acres for the garden, the long driveway and red brick of the seventy-year-old single-story ranch house loomed in the distance. Jennette started rehearsing. *Car repair and rent, car repair and rent.*

"Oh dear, you look wonderful." Aunt Faye gripped her in a hug and smooched her cheek.

"Thank you, Auntie." She had showered and changed into nice clothes.

"Who goes there?"

Jen looked over at the easy chair that Uncle Rob was always dutifully holding down and was greeted with the likeness of a hairy, goat troll in bib overalls.

"Oh, Robert take that silly mask off." Faye rolled her eyes at her husband and shooed Jen in past the foyer. "I made fresh tea, would you like a drink? It's hot today."

"How's my niece, still working at Lou's Diner?" Like most old men, Uncle Rob went right for a person's job situation. He stood up slowly and pulled off his mask, giving Jen a typical uncle side hug.

"You bet Uncle Rob. I'll be there until people find something better to do with their money than spending it on food." Jen sat on the leather loveseat, placing her keys next to her, where she knew they expected a husband to be.

"What brings you over on this steamy summer evening dear?" Aunt Faye handed Jen a tall glass full of ice cubes and unsweetened Lipton tea.

"I hate coming over under these circumstances, but I've hit a rough patch." Jennette looked at the floor and took in a slow deep breath. "I need money."

"Please tell me you're not using again," Faye avoided looking at her and glanced over at Rob who was nervously fumbling with his eyeglasses.

"It's not that, I just..." Jen paused, thinking of her rehearsal. Her eyes searched for a distraction on the walls and stopped at the crucifix over the piano where she had sat many times on her Aunt's lap as she rehearsed for church. Below it, a plaque read in bold letters 'For God so loved the world that he gave his only begotten Son.' Jen put her hand across her stomach and had a sudden memory from biology class, 'At six weeks the head and face are forming.' Her plan was falling apart. Her Aunt and Uncle had no children. Faye had endometriosis and couldn't conceive. "I'm pregnant." The words fell out of her mouth. She kept her eyes on the floor, feeling the tears welling up.

Faye walked over and sat next to Jennette, hooking an arm around her as they both cried. "It's a miracle dear, you've been blessed."

"It's a curse. I can't do this now. Not where I am in life. I can't raise a child." Her thoughts drifted to yesterday when she was wanting a fix.

"Your Uncle and I have talked about this. We would like to adopt your child. You just have to take care of yourself and bring the pregnancy to term." Faye stroked Jen's hair trying to look at her face.

The words sunk in. Give up your baby. Nurture and grow a life inside of your body for nine months and give them to someone else. Then, the words seemed strange in her mind, just a few hours ago she had convinced herself the thing inside her was no more than a cluster of cells, now she was assigning it a pronoun.

"We can help with the finances dear. You need proper prenatal care, and regular visits with an OBGYN." Uncle Rob piped up from his usual quiet self.

"You can come over whenever you want. If the time is right we will tell them you are their mother." Faye's gentle green eyes twinkled with hope.

"I don't know. I guess I have a decision to make."

"We all love you, Jen, just remember that."

Jen stood up to leave, she felt numb and hollow. She had a weight on her now, an unbearable force. She now felt a responsibility beyond herself. A potential new life depended on her.

The drive home was full of nerves. *Watch out for*

deer. Self-preservation had boiled to the front of her brain. The thought of stopping for some junk food at the convenience store hit her. *But what about...it.*

The next few weeks were painful, Jennette agonized over simple choices every day. Should she drink tap water, soda, or anything with sugar? She googled every food choice, and buying things at the grocery store became a field of landmines. On her first visit, the doctor insisted on a sonogram and gave her a prescription for prenatal vitamins.

She started feeling flutters in her womb, a primordial mammal was flipping and swimming inside a sack of fluid between her hip bones. She watched Alien, the movie again, Ridley Scott's adaptation of 'you gave birth to the worst critter ever.' Maybe natural childbirth wasn't so bad.

Her call to Auntie Faye went well, "I've decided to accept your offer. I will go through with the pregnancy."

"Oh, Jenny! This is the best decision. You won't be disappointed," Faye invited her over and explained the legal aspects of the arrangement. Adoption and abortion, the words were so close yet not.

Each ultrasound revealed a little more. All parties decided to not divulge the sex of the child until birth. A healthy human was not easy to construct. After the morning sickness subsided the perpetual hunger started. The weight gain that ensued was eventually recognized as a pregnancy by

Jennette's customers. She tried to deflect the dad and due date questions.

Fall passed and Christmas came, she was through the second trimester. They would wake when she slept, and sleep while she was awake. It was a 24/7 job with no paycheck. She had thrown the bathroom scale in a closet after so much weight gain. *How could a five-pound baby make you weigh forty more pounds?* Then came cankles and the days of 'I only wear long dresses and loose tops.'

At some point buying clothes became farcical. Her nipples were always sore and tender, and her hips expanded into celestial dimensions. The nightly ritual of this giant thing pressed into her skin, shifting and squirming inside her made horror films mild by comparison. The trips to the bathroom became so frequent she wanted a port-a-potty in the bedroom. How they knew how to kick her bladder over and over for a little extra room for themselves was a mystery.

Yet the due date approached, it was near Easter, and Mom and Auntie insisted on a small baby shower.

"Have you thought of names Auntie?"

"Don't you want to name them?"

"No, if anything we should decide together."

"How about Madison? It can be a boy or girl's name and means 'Son of Matthew' with Matthew meaning 'Gift from God.'"

"I like Madison." Jen wrapped an arm around her bulbous belly as the baby shifted inside her. She finished the second piece of fudge cake and ice cream.

The last sonogram signaled that cervical ripening was imminent. The nurse said, "When the contractions are less than ten minutes apart, head to the emergency room."

The following Saturday, Jennette had been off work most of the week. Uncle Rob offered to help with her bills.

When her Aunt and Uncle picked her up it was late, but her contractions had started and were getting closer together. "You know tomorrow is Palm Sunday?"

"What does that mean." Jen was tensed up from the pain. Her body was preparing for birth on its own. She was merely a vessel now.

"It's the day Jerusalem welcomes Jesus. The people laid down palm fronds so his donkey would not have to step on the ground."

"I need an epidural, not palm leaves." Jen laid back in the bucket seat until they reached the hospital.

"Oh wow! You are fully dilated, we don't have time to administer an epidural, you're going to have to tough this one out sister." The nurse finished her exam in the emergency room and said, "Natural childbirth."

Later in the birthing room after an hour of pushing, Jen laying there in her birthday suit sat up and exclaimed, "Somebody better help me!"

The doctor sat up and said, "Cavalry is on the way!" and performed an episiotomy with his shears.

One push later, Madison was born into this world.

TEA AT TIFFANY'S

By Kevin Marlow

An eager sun crested the horizon, its heated spears daggered the frosty landscape like low-vibration fiery tongues. Rays melted a dense layer of frost on the metal fascia above the eastern window of an unremarkable ranch dwelling near the west side of anywhere. Splashes of droplets dripping down onto the ledge of the window enticed a thirsty gray and white tufted titmouse. The little bird flitted down to the window sill for a sip from the drips, a difficult find in the cold regions during the gripping winter months. Its drumming wings brushed the window and woke the old man in the bed beyond the glazed glass.

Rubbing his eyes and fumbling for his spectacles, Charles had never shunned waking early, a vestigial ritual from early days on the farm that never died. "Marybeth, what day is it?"

The door to the bath, which had been painted too many times, creaked as the hinges sang to life, a waif of an elderly silver-haired woman slid into the frame. "I told you last night, it is the day we go for Tea at Tiffany's."

"I meant what day of the week." His grumpy tone was reinforced by the thud of calloused heels on tongue and groove oak hardwood floor, its brown, shellacked surface polished for a hundred years by bare feet.

"It's Sunday dear, so dress in your finest."

"I thought Tea at Tiffany's was a joke. I remember hearing Uncle Joe ribbing people at our family gatherings, he would say, 'Oh, you just wait till you get your Tea at Tiffany's.'"

"It has become a bit of a tale, but it is a real thing, Charles." Marybeth wrapped her slender arms around the heft of a gut that had mined, farmed, butchered, and labored his family out of poverty for decades.

"Real or not, I've never looked forward to sipping hot tea like a royal at some fancy tea house. I like my tea cold and unsweetened like we had on the farm." Charles ran his stout fingers through her hair as she lay it briefly against his barrel chest.

He turned to the closet and stopped. Marybeth had not set out clothes for him in years, yet there, next to the wardrobe, was his dress shirt, the one with buttons on the collar to hold the tie. Black suit pants and a lonely necktie were hanging neatly as well.

Grabbing a towel he headed to the washroom to

take a shower. The cold of the claw foot cast iron tub was contrasted with the heat of the water. As the steam billowed into the air and droplets condensed on the window, the water washed over Charles till he was clean as a newborn.

Buttoning up the shirt in front of the mirror, Charles felt as if he was looking at someone else as if a touch of youth had returned and transformed him somehow. Thin black socks slid into fine leather oxfords that had been polished once or twice a year for weddings and funerals. Folding up his collar and flipping the red striped tie around his neck, he struggled as usual with the half Windsor knot. It usually took a few times to get the length just right.

Walking into the main room of the house, the ancient wooden clock his grandfather had brought from Germany, ticked away life's seconds. Charles found Marybeth looking at the wall, wiping tears from her eyes with a tissue. She was staring at their wedding picture, the one that had been in the same spot for forty-nine and one-half years. He wanted to say something, yet over the years it had all been said, and more. She turned and walked toward the coat rack by the door, her eyes avoiding his for some reason. Usually, she would have remarked how handsome he was in his Sunday best outfit.

Charles jabbed his arms into a double-breasted black trench coat, buttoned it down, and lashed the belt closed, the bite of winter had arrived some time ago. Walking silently through the neighborhood where their three children had learned to run, ride bikes, and wrestle, Charles wasn't sure which was the tea house, only that it was past the church in an old dining hall.

Nearing the square, a booming voice was reverberating, bouncing off red brick walls and concrete walkways. A small crowd was gathered around a tall man in plain black garments with a white clerical collar, gesticulating and talking loudly.

"Crush their hearts of stone! Let the indecision crumble away, only then will the truth be revealed. Peel away the layers. Cast off the tattered husk of the material world, because inside is the sacred heart, the essence of what we are. What we need lies within, it is up to us as individuals to find it." As the man spoke in mighty baritone, the light of the sun crawled across the square, its warmth a welcome respite from the chilled breeze that was whipping the long coats and scarves of the small gathering.

Listening to the impromptu sermon, Marybeth's arm laced in his, Charles' mind drifted back a few weeks.

"What's wrong grandpa?" Golden eyes of crystal peered into his with concern.

"Nothing Sis, I just haven't felt the best lately." Sam bounded down the hallway to fess up to grandma, nothing ever made it past Samantha.

Charles rubbed his shoulder and downed the rest of his black coffee. Looking across the room,

Mason was twirling around on his knees, spinning a red and white 1965 die-cast corvette, vibrating his lips for motor noises. The pain had been crawling into his chest for some time, like a knife it reached from his shoulder to his sternum.

Marybeth marched into the room and led Samantha and Mason to the kitchen, setting out a plate of homemade chocolate chip cookies and two glasses of whole white milk. Walking back into the living room, she folded her arms and lowered her eyebrows, waiting for an explanation.

"What?" Charles' derisive tone only served to calcify Marybeth's attitude. Grandpa Charles as they called him, didn't like his precious time with grandchildren interrupted.

"If that child can tell something is wrong, you need to tell me what's going on. I will call your doctor for an appointment tomorrow." Marybeth put a palm on his forehead and felt the pulse in his neck.

"Your heart is pounding like a jazz drummer on cocaine."

"It's the AFib. I took my meds this morning." He wiped his eyes and yawned, handing his wife an empty stained coffee mug.

"I'll call the nurse in the morning." She turned to take the cup to the kitchen and check on the little ones.

Ave Maria! Ave Maria Mater Dei!

A piercing female soprano voice pulled Charles from his ruminations. The sidewalk preacher's voice had been supplanted by a choir.

"Is it still Christmas?" Charles turned to Marybeth with a befuddled look.

"You'll see. Let's follow the sound of the choir." Walking further past the square, the clang of bells rang out from the brick tower a few blocks down. The sound of the choir was soaring above the bells ringing as the sun illuminated the belfry.

"Should we go to the church?"

"The ceremony is just now ending, besides, we have to meet for Tea at Tiffany's, have you forgotten?" Marybeth smiled and looked in the morning light twenty years younger; Charles smiled back and kept walking.

They crossed a park, dotted with fruit trees stripped bare by fall and followed a winding stone walkway, past statues of St. Francis of Assisi and the Virgin Mary. At the end of the path, a large building rose from the hillside, its red cedar wooden siding punctuated by stained glass windows that were dancing with light and movement. Below the ornamental panels, each pane was decorated with beveled glass and etchings, the eternal flame, the dove of peace, and a cup overflowing.

Marybeth had turned and looked on as Charles gazed in wonder. The stairs to the door beckoned as they watched the sun ignite the orange clay tile roof like fire. Reaching the door, a concierge pulled the winter coat from his shoulders, opened the french door, and motioned for him to enter.

"Welcome home Charles." His eldest sister had come and wrapped her arms around him.

Charles looked around in confusion. He had lost Dot to cancer five years ago. He looked at her. She did not appear to be a day over thirty. "How? What, what's going on?"

"We've been waiting so long to see you again. You remember Michael?" His friend from childhood marched up, not a day over sixteen years old when he died of polio, and shook his hand with vigor.

"Where's Marybeth?" Charles turned and caught her waving through the glass from outside as she walked back down the stairs to the park.

"Some need help crossing over, you don't remember, but you had a massive heart attack last night. There was nothing anyone could do. Uncle Joe is here, but I don't think you need him to explain what having Tea at Tiffany's is about. Do you want milk or sugar? We have so much to talk about. Do you like honey?"

THE SABINARATH OF XENOSCYTHE

By Kevin Marlow

"I'm afraid we can't let that happen."

"Why?" Tokarov hadn't cared much about leaving until confronted with the possibility he couldn't.

"You know the answer you just don't want to admit it," The Overlord's voice boomed in his head.

"Admit what?" A sinking feeling gripped his gut.

"It, the giant in the room so to speak. I want you to say it."

"Say what?" Tokarov gritted his teeth.

"Answer your own question."

"I'm never going to win because I'm a failure," He knew it was what had to be said.

"Not *just* a failure, like your planet, finish the thought."

"I'm an anachronism, a vestige of a bygone era, a living fossil," Admitting it stung. Having been OK with just surviving for the past months, the reality of never escaping enraged him.

"And?"

"Fossils are to be harvested and studied...in the labyrinth."

"Precisely. If you are allowed safe passage, well you know we will have to let them all out, Hmmm?"

"Alright, I get it. What is my next assignment?"

"You have to capture the Sabinarath."

"So, I get the suicide mission. I thought you needed me?"

"Like everyone on Xenoscythe you too are...expendable."

Tokarov reinserted the tubes in his nose and adjusted his mouthpiece, shifting the oxygen generator on his pack for comfort, he flipped the light on his visor to high and took off in a steady jog down the new tunnel. The rock floor was worn smooth by thousands of feet over the centuries. The clunk of his protective boots echoed off the walls. He had never seen the Sabinarath but heard tales of its lair, a pit hidden by piles of bones of foolish men and boys. A creature born to destroy dreams and crush souls. Some called it the 'Evil One', too scared to even utter its name.

The ribs of the passageway widened gradually into a vast cavern dotted with ochre rock formations and shallow pools of the acrid groundwater they all drank. Tokarov slowed to a walk and knelt by a pool to replenish his canteen. He removed his mouthpiece and sipped the mineral water. It burned as he swished it in his mouth.

Taking in a breath, he tasted oxygen. Removing the respirator, he drank in the fresh air, glad to be free of the breathing apparatus, if only for a short time.

Hearing distant footfalls and banter, Tokarov ducked behind a large boulder and drew his dagger. Three distinct voices reverberated in the alcove. Waiting for them he calculated the risk of confronting them. His rations were depleted, and there was an unwritten rule among the denizens of the underground maze that none in the competition should go hungry. Gripping his knife he belted out a greeting as they passed the rock.

"Aye!"

The men turned to Tokarov, placing hands on their weapon hilts. "To whom do we have the pleasure?"

Holstering his steel, he spoke, "I'm Tokarov."

"I'm Alpha, the old man here we call Omega, the youngster is named Ego," Alpha took the lead and reached out with his hand open, an ancient gesture that reinforced the idea he brandished no weapon.

Taking his hand with a firm grip, Tokarov locked emerald eyes on him, "I need sustenance, I ran out of food yesterday."

"We were making our way to the nearest shaft;

our captors dropped a pallet of rations two days ago. There should be plenty left if you care to join our group. Strength in numbers, eh?"

The men walked to the delivery shaft to conserve their energy, stabbing the dark ahead with their headlamps. They had to be careful, Grigglesneeds were known to ambush people when they obtained food. A nasty race of reptilian humanoids, they preferred the taste of humans over rations.

Ego spoke first, "What brings you to this lovely corner of hell?"

"I bested the last trial and was granted passage. Killing two doppelgangers was no easy feat, but The Overlords kept their word and allowed me to progress," Tokarov brushed a shock of sweaty dark curls from in front of his eyes.

"Our group consisted of twelve originally. We three are the only ones left; the others were slain by the Bog Wraith at our last trial. Since then we have wandered the catacombs waiting to be called up again," Alpha turned his iron jaw toward Tokarov, gauging his reaction.

"Has anyone told you what happens if one makes it through the next trial?"

Ego slipped a chuckle, "Some say freedom, others death. Either would be a relief to me. Living underground like a grub worm has worn a hole in my soul."

Tokarov shot a glance at his new companions; Omega's wry smile seemed out of place. The light from the delivery shaft was glowing ahead in the passage. Boxes and packs of rations were scattered about, their yellow mylar pouches reflected in the light.

"Grab at least enough for a few days, the next shaft is miles away," Alpha and his crew stuffed their backpacks with the meals. Tokarov stacked the food neatly into the main compartment on his rucksack, taking enough for a week.

"There is a table rock further up the cave; we can stop and eat there," Alpha pointed into the darkness ahead. Standing around the flat stone, the four pulled off their packs and dug out their meals and utensils. Tokarov pulled a chow set out of his side pocket on his pack. The knife, fork, and spoon were locked together, The Overlord's crest stamped deep into the metal. Pulling the spoon from the set, he gave thanks and cut a pouch open with his blade. Alpha closed his eyes and bowed his head, invisible words dancing on his lips as he pulled apart a dense slice of white bread. Looking on, Ego's dismissive giggle was cut short by a steely glance from Omega. Tokarov spooned the gruel out of the pouch, mushing it with his teeth.

"There is a safe haven a half mile from here. We were headed there when we found you. Would you care to join us?" Alpha heaved his rucksack onto his back and looked at the new acquaintance.

"Not sure where I'm headed," Tokarov decided to follow along for now. He knew of a few safe places in the caverns, finding another would be prudent.

They trudged in silence, the food percolating in their bellies. A split in the path caused the three to veer left to the larger more well-traveled passage. Stopping Tokarov looked to the right. A thick powdery spider web draped across the middle of the opening. Undisturbed dirt, like dust, blanketed the ground. Squinting, it almost looked like a bare footprint had been there from some time ago.

"I'm looking for something, I'm going down the trail less trampled," He dared not mention his mission to find the Sabinarath. Knowing the beast's reputation, saying such could lead to a confrontation.

"Be well brother, maybe we will see you on the other side," The troupe shuffled off towards safety.

Tokarov pulled his dagger out and cut the web from the entry. Putting his lamp on low, he stepped into the darkness. The cave seemed to narrow with each step until it stopped at a narrow slit. Debating whether to turn around, he noticed a cool breeze brush his cheek. Pulling off his respirator and inhaling, a fresh effervescent earthy scent greeted his nostrils. Squeezing through the gap, he followed his nose. After a few hundred feet the cave widened again, and the dry rocky floor gave way to damp clay. Reaching down, he dug in his fingertips and crumbled the soil in his palm.

Picking up his pace, he hoped it was an oasis, a rumored place in the vast caverns fed by light and moisture through deep cracks in the crust of the planet. Looking at the walls of the cave, spots of phosphorescent green algae were speckled in clumps. The cavern opened ahead, a soft blue glow ringing the rocks in a corona. Walking through it, he caught his breath.

Swallows were swirling in circles above him, tittering. The roof of the vast cathedral-like opening was cracked in the shape of lightning bolts, the glow of Aerialis, a sun that never set on the surface of Xenoscythe burst through the crevices, shining down on vast carpets of brilliant orange and green moss, dotted with massive ferns. An outcrop of igneous rock jutted over a vast lake the color of polished sapphire gems. The rocks were alive with multitudes of orchids and flowering, hanging plants, a plethora of life he had not seen since the Earth had died and been harvested by Xenoscythe Overlords.

Walking over to the edge of the water, Tokarov cupped his hands and smelled it, touching it to his lips and tongue. Dumping the putrid contents of his canteen, he dipped it in the water and filled it. Rubbing the fresh water on his filthy face with calloused hands tipped by dirty fingernails, he was suddenly confronted with how he looked gazing into the reflective surface of the water. He hadn't bathed in months; grit and dust ringed the areas on his face around where the respirator lay on his skin.

Afraid it was all a lucid dream, he decided to clean himself and his clothes before he woke up. Even the dream of a bath was better than the endless caverns and rock. Dropping his backpack away from the shore on a sleeping mat, Tokarov endeavored to clean his garments first. Stripping naked, he found a sandstone rock to scrub the garrison shirt and breeches. Thrashing them about in the crystal clear water, he marveled at his arms flexing. The scarcity of food had chiseled his frame to muscle and bone. Youth provided mere patches of dark curly body hair. He smiled for the first time in weeks, feeling good about himself.

Throwing his clothes over a few woody bushes to dry, the water drew him in for a swim. Standing in waist-deep water, his bare feet massaged by tiny pebbles, he watched a serpent swim past. Its triangular head dodged back and forth with a frog in its mouth, wheezing, pierced by the fangs. Diving under the water, he felt the filth of his situation dissolving into the water. Swimming until he couldn't touch toes with his head above water, he no longer felt imprisoned. He treaded water naked, the cool water splashing and plastering his long dark curls to his skull.

Wiggling a now clean fingertip in his ear canal, he craned his head. The distinct trill of a soprano human voice rippled across the lake. Fearing he might drown like a sailor drawn to the sirens, he swam back to the shore and resolved to use a piece of flint and his blade to burn some driftwood and investigate the sound later when he was dry and dressed. The sound was so ethereal and distant that he wasn't sure if it was merely a hallucination.

The fire popped and crackled, the embers curling and dying as thin wisps of smoke wafted into the air of a cave whose cracks had dimmed as the sun Aerialis dipped low to the horizon. Roasting some striped yellow fruit on a stick, it was the only fresh food he had in months. Peeling it, the charred flesh was stringy with pulpy seeds and tasted vaguely of bananas and kiwis.

With a full belly and clean clothes, Tokarov almost felt human again. Real, non-cybernetic humans were near extinction. The Overlords deemed them a threat since they had destroyed the Earth with their nascent technology. Testing their ability to survive with other orphaned aliens led to the Trials of Xenoscythe. If they wanted to prove themselves worthy of survival, they must win in the trials.

Tokarov had no choice but to sleep. The swim drained his energy, he snuggled in his survival blanket, as his mind drifted back to the song floating across the lake. He sank like a stone in ether. The insects sawed at the silence lulling him to slumber.

The chirping of birds woke him. Opening his eye he was greeted with a purple iris, ringed in long dark lashes, hovering centimeters from his. Reaching for the dagger under his sleeping mat, he crab-walked backward away from the interloper. She giggled at this, putting slender marble fingers over a coy smile.

"Hello, what is your name?" What appeared to be a human female straightened to a languid pose with hands on hips, her angular form draped in a loose-fitting robe. Burgundy curls fell around a face with high cheekbones and full lips.

"I'm Tokarov, who are you?" He pulled on his boots and studied her frame. Her breast-to-hip ratio was near perfect, her shoulders didn't slump, and her arms were long with toned muscles.

"Call me Lora Lei," She reached a hand down and helped Tokarov to his feet.

"I thought I heard singing yesterday. I assume that was you," He sheathed the blade and tucked it in his belt.

"When I stand naked under the waterfall, something comes over me, crashing in waves through my body. I make sounds when I feel pleasure," The slow closing of her eyes sent shivers through him.

"Follow me," She turned and curled an index finger, winking.

Leading him on a trail around the lake, they reached a grove of primordial fruit trees. The sweet scent of blossoms and flowers was intoxicating to a man that had been denied the presence of most living things for months.

"Just pick one. They all taste good in their own unique way."

Tokarov fondled a pomegranate, slicing the skin with his knife and popping the tart swelled seed pods into his mouth. He grunted in approval.

She trembled when he grunted again, making animal noises as he ate. She looked at her hand and felt the claws aching to grow out. *Not yet.*

Walking over behind him, she reached down and grabbed him. He swallowed rough and hurled the bitten fruit into the grove, turning and reaching down he clutched her posterior. They could feel the match of their curves collapsing into each other in the proper places. Their mouths intertwined like snakes dancing to death.

Wrapping around each other, she ached as he grinded his muscular frame into hers. The right time never came, she was robbed of her opportunity as he drained them both in a simultaneous wrack of shudders.

She rolled over on the grass next to him and let out a sigh, looking at her hand, realizing she no longer had the strength to morph into the Sabinarath and devour him. Yet she had his seed; she could harbor it for quite some time. Tokarov stared up at the glowing roof of the cave, hoping he had just ensured the genesis of a future human, not even realizing there had never been a non-altered human with purple eyes or an oasis on a dead planet.

His thought of self-preservation returned; dressing he turned to the trail and thought of the trials. Alpha, Omega, and Ego were waiting for him at the safe haven.

As he hiked, the telepathy of The Overlord cracked his mind, "What of the creature? Did you find it?" He sounded impatient.

"No. I found nothing," Tokarov had learned to hide things to stay alive.

"This will delay your next trial."

"So be it." The good and bad often felt the same these days.

THE TRIAL OF TOKAROV

By Kevin Marlow

As Tokarov made his way back to the cavern, a smile dotted his lips. Nothing so strange had ever happened to him. He had never made love to a stranger before, yet here on Xenoscythe, it came to him naturally. He sniffed the curls of hair hanging around his face; a faint flowery scent still lingered. If such beautiful females could be found in these caverns, he thought it might be acceptable to be trapped in the labyrinth after all.

Exiting the small cave opening, he followed bootprints to find his new acquaintances. A moment of regret caught him, and he stopped before strapping the respirator back on his face. Turning around, he wanted something as proof of his encounter. Nearing the split in the caverns, he didn't remember the turn. Sure the opening was near, yet he was confronted with more stone. The lack of oxygen made him light-headed. Sure he had passed the alcove, he turned around and broke into a jog, flipping the beam on his headlamp to high. He stopped, huffing as the stale air of the cave coated his lungs like spiderwebs. Desperate for oxygen, he threaded the tubes back into his nostrils and sucked on the mouthpiece, turning the breathing machine to its highest setting and slumping down with his bottom to the floor.

He now wondered if the maze itself was an undulating moving creature, one that could change shape. Maybe he was trapped in the intestines of some vast inter-dimensional alien; one whose rock was like living tissue. Either way, he needed to find the safe haven. His dagger wouldn't be much use against a group of marauding aliens.

Working his way up to a steady run, the rucksack shifted back and forth on his shoulders. He drew in ragged breaths from the oxygen concentrator, the slapping of the boot's treads echoing in his ears. The light danced to and fro in a rhythmic motion as he found his pace, and sweat dribbled from his brow, stinging his eyes.

Ahead an eerie green glow around the walls signaled an opening to a larger lighted space. Tokarov slowed to a walk, the wheezing of his exhales pulsing out of the apparatus tangled with his long hair. The vast room was illuminated by clumps of gelatinous blobs clinging to the ribs and ceiling of the space. The walls were chiseled into semi-smooth surfaces.

Enraptured by the glow, he walked over to investigate. Leaning in close, he observed a barely perceptible movement, the globs leaving behind iridescent trails of slime. They were alive, some sort of bioluminescent jelly, so many of them the room glowed a soft chartreuse color.

"Funny little creatures aren't they?" Tokarov jumped as a firm hand gripped his shoulder. Looking back, Omega's wide grin welcomed him.

"Bizarre life forms for sure, on Earth these were usually found deep in the bottom of the ocean."

"I know. These almost seem the product of some experimentation, not the work of a...diety."

The words caused him to snap back, locking into Omega's sharp gray eyes.

"Come, we have things to discuss." Omega motioned for Tokarov to follow. Leading him over to chairs carved of stone, he waved a hand for him to have a seat. Alpha and Ego were already sitting down, holding their steel canteen cups. The room was immense; other groups of humans were gathered in clusters. The muffled din of conversations echoed off the rock.

"Did you find what you were looking for?" Ego piped up, his words firm like leather.

"No, not exactly," Tokarov sensed bitterness in the tone of Ego's voice.

"He's lying. I can see it in his aura," Alpha surmised as Ego stared hard at Tokarov.

Omega, being the peacemaker spoke up, "Before we can allow you to join us, you have to tell us what you found."

"I found an oasis, and a female companion," Tokarov's nerves quivered in the tenor of his words.

Ego's head jerked, slapped by the tone of Tokarov's voice, "There are no females in the Labyrinth. You were tricked. Did you consummate the union?"

"We, uh, I don't know."

"LIES!" Ego reached for his dagger. Stunned, Tokarov stood, ready to defend himself.

"If the Sabinarath has your seed, we will go to trial," Omega said in an ominous tone.

Tokarov went blank. What kind of magic was he dealing with? The siren song drifted into his mind; the garden like Eden, the serpent, Alpha, Omega. His epiphany was sudden and sent an electrical shock through his frame, "Your, Him........How?"

Omega's eyes swirled with twisting colors, "I don't have the powers I used to possess. I have been transfigured back to human form, Alpha is my son. I am who has always been."

"Then why are you here?" Tokarov said in palpable confusion.

"I was the Deity of Earth alone when they harvested it. The Overlords of Xenoscythe took most of my powers and banished me to the maze, so that I may be tested as well. You and all humans were made in my image, and to that form, I have returned." Tokarov fell back to his seat.

Ego took his hand from his dagger and spoke, "I want proof. None have lived after seeing the Sabinarath."

"The water. I have water from the lake where we..."

Ego held out his cup. Tokarov pulled his canteen from his pack and poured the precious water into the cup.

Ego groaned and shuddered as he gulped the water down, "The well of life itself," He slammed the steel vessel onto the rock and trembled as if waiting for a scream, emotions washing over him.

Calming himself, Ego turned to Tokarov and glowered at him.

"You are not the first to be tricked by the Sabinarath," Omega tried to break the tension.

"So what happens now?" Tokarov turned to the elder with an inquisitive look.

"The Overlords of Xenoscythe will have trials."

"What will we have to do in the trials?"

"Survive."

* * *

The roar of the observers deafened everyone. Aliens and humanoids stomped and clapped, hollering in a din that drowned out all extraneous sounds. Tokarov gripped the metal bars of his enclosure and stared down onto the battleground. He had been roused from sleep and separated from the others many hours ago. Looking up the cavern walls, spectators stretched in levels a dozen units above him.

"The Trial begins!" A baritone voice boomed over the noise. A thunderous din of feet stomping and cacophonous yells and shrieks erupted. The reptilian hand of a Grigglesneed slipped a steel cuff onto Tokarov's wrist, handing him an iron buckler. The small shield locked onto the cuff on his weak hand. A loop on the handcuff was threaded with a large chain, stout enough to fell a tree.

Without warning, the giant reptilian humanoid jerked the chain and Tokarov had no choice but to follow or be dragged down the floor of the dripping rough-hewn passage. Torches flickered, illuminating the rough stone of the walls, gargoyles dangled from the bottom of the lamp bases, wide mouths grinning with pointed teeth and outstretched tongues.

Circled flights of stone stairs led to the bottom of the tower. A beefy guard stood at the gate, brandishing a long hardwood shaft topped with a metal ball, engraved on three sides with faces, each one representing a face of the fates, Clotho, Lachesis, and Atropos.

The voice boomed again, "A god must best his creation, deity versus mortal!"

Tokarov looked across the floor of the arena

as another colossus lowered a helm over Omega's square jaw, a shield and the chain dropping from his arm as well. The guard handed Tokarov the mace adorned with the fates and opened the gate. Omega and Tokarov walked toward each other to the center of the pitch. The chains were locked together, a mere ten feet of log chain separating the two. The helmets hid their faces, each twirled a mace and tested the tension on the chain.

Omega made the first move jerking the chain between them, trying to pull Tokarov from his feet. The mortal had youth in his step and hopped when he pulled, heaving the weapon behind his back and over his shoulder aiming for Omega's helmet. Sensing his move, the old one dodged aside as the iron bounced off the stone, sending sparks flying as a roar sailed up from the crowd.

The two circled each other, the tension in the chain grinding and chinking as the spectators grew restless. Tokarov pulled the chain closer, jumping links as he closed the gap to Omega. Feeling his advantage was in tight melee, he gritted his teeth and dragged Omega closer. Pulling with a final heave, Tokarov clenched his gut and swung in a windmill fashion over his head. In a sudden defensive move, Omega felt slack in the chain and hoisted the buckler over his head. Tokarov's blow glanced off the shield, cleaving off a chunk of the metal, showering sparks.

The crowd erupted with the fires of the battle.

Omega backed off as Tokarov pulled the battle mace over his shoulder, panting from exertion. The mortal realized this was final. If killed by a god, he was doomed to be the unremembered, a faceless passerby of the cosmos, a nameless nobody.

The image of Lora Lei bloomed in his mind. The thought of another taking her from him, even a god, boiled the anger in his soul. The injustice of his childhood stood in his way. Wasn't that also the fault of some unnamed god? A fire erupted in his body; he must kill the god responsible for his pain.

Blood flowed to his hands and feet as anger boiled the fluid in his limbs. A hatred he had never connected with gave renewed life to his body. The mace whistled back and forth in a cross-motion over his head as he stomped toward and stalked Omega. The patrons of the arena, sensing his resolve, came to life, cheering him on. One blow shattered the chain between them. Cutting off the ring he chiseled the arena down to a corner. The old one stood defiantly, raising his shield and mace. Tokarov, fueled by a lifetime of pain and regrets, funneled all his energy into a single blow that tore Omega's head off, helm and all. As it tumbled to the stone, the blood gushing onto the arena floor, the roar of the crowds filled the tower.

* * *

"Tell me more."

Tokarov sighed as he propped his head up from the lush green carpet of grass, "Why?"

"I need to know why you are the one."

"The one?" Tokarov snorted in derision. He had lovers back on Earth.

"We are tasked with creating a new race that will thrive in the terraformation of Xenoscythe," Brushing back curly locks, Lora Lei plucked a small pink daisy flower head and spun it under her nose, inhaling the robust scent, "Tell me about your life back on Earth."

"We were farmers. Our crops were dying by degrees each year. At first, it was just the extreme weather, but then the plants themselves began to fail. As the atmosphere thinned the radiation from space distorted their DNA, crippling their ability to thrive and produce viable generations," Tokarov looked across the calm blue water, his mind drifting into the past.

"I sensed your life force when you first arrived in the labyrinth. My omnipresence on Xenoscythe allows me to observe the planet on a spiritual level, yet I can't see memories."

"Memories are all I have left."

"I want to know about your childhood. What kind of world was it?"

"Our family was isolated. We holed up at the edge of what was left of civilization and made our stand. My parents believed in survival of the fittest. They pitted siblings and cousins against each other, hoping to make us strong."

"Did it?"

"Of course not. The older ones abused the others; we learned to hide our strengths and disguise our abilities. If one stood out, they were beaten down and humiliated in front of the others."

"How were you chosen? The Overlords kill most survivors when they harvest a planet," She reached over and drew her nails over his torso, causing him shivers and goose flesh.

"I don't know. I've always had a mental antenna for the stranger things. I dreamt about a giant transport ship, larger than our solar system. We all knew the planet was dying. Most of the humans were like the ancient one Nero, fiddling as Rome burned. I began meditating and started a communion with The Overlords of Xenoscythe. I didn't know them as such then, as a young man, but I knew the end was near," The Sabinarath tried to pry open a telepathic channel into Tokarov's mind. He felt the intrusion and walled off his subconscious, cracking a smile as she continued caressing him.

"You are strong. I know why they chose you. Your mind is a vise, your body is hard and fertile. These are the qualities a new race of beings will need," Lora lay her head close to his neck, her hot breath pulsing on his neck, "You know I am not limited to one offspring."

Tokarov tensed up, "What is this place? How do we fulfill our obligations and leave here?"

"We are in one of the many wombs of Xenoscythe. Others like us are bound to procreate, lest we all perish on this infernal rock."

His eyes shifted around, the sun Aerialis glowed from cracks in the roof of the cave, glinting off the moisture beaded on white orchid flowers and orange moss dangling from the walls of rock. A tiny gold-breasted finch flitted to a bare branch near them, trilling, cocking its head from side to side.

"I let you in. I could have let you perish at the claws of countless alien hordes," Her purple eyes closed, brushing the skin on his neck with her eyelashes.

"But, you didn't and here we are," Tokarov ran his fingers through her tangled curls. Looking over, the soft light of the cavern gave her hair a hue like the heart of ancient redwood trees he had seen on vacation as a small child. Curling his arm around her shoulder, they pieced together like an organic puzzle, "Exactly how does an alien give birth?"

"We give ourselves up," Lora Lei leaned up on her arm, staring at Tokarov.

"For how long? On Earth, it takes a mother twenty or so years to create a viable offspring."

"The Sabinarath gives itself up at birth. Females are no longer needed except for gestation. I can give you more than one if you wish."

"What do you mean by gives itself up?"

"We perish. Our life force is passed on to the

future generation."

"What happens to me?" Tokarov's heart galloped. He suddenly felt the gravity of it all.

"You are left to rear the progeny. It is the order of things."

"But, what about nursing, nurturing? What about teaching the basics of living?"

"You will be a good parent, I just know it," She brushed her lips on his neck. The burn of her touch radiated down through his limbs and fingers. An aching fear gripped Tokarov.

His mind shot backward through his memories to his childhood, to the screaming and fighting. Endless crying spells often stretched into an unfathomable depression that yawned for months at a time.

"What if I want out? What if I refuse the adjudication of the trials?"

Lora Lei reached her hand and cupped it around his neck, whispering, "Close your eyes and I will show you."

Tokarov closed his eyes. He felt the strength in her grasp. Her fingers began to lengthen into clawed appendages, covered in iridescent turquoise scales. The grip strengthened and rotated his head towards her. Her mouth and nose merged, elongating into a massive beak-like protuberance lined with tiny razor-like grooves. The beautiful purple irises enlarged into discs the size of dinner plates. Rows of feather-like hair grew out of the now bird-like face. A forked tongue split its beak and danced across his face, tickling it. With the force of a steel trap, in his mind meld, it snapped off his head and he jerked back into reality.

"You're going to eat me?" He was incredulous.

"I must abort your seed and seek a new surrogate if you break the ruling of The Overlord's trial."

"It doesn't exactly leave me many options does it?"

"No. There is one other contingency I must confess," Her skin glowed and rippled from the reflections of the water undulating on the cave walls, "I must feed as the Sabinarath each week to grow our offspring."

"I'm guessing the native reptiles and amphibians of this area won't do."

"No. When the sun Aerialis is at its zenith each week, I must transform and feed, otherwise, our hybrid offspring will die."

"I'm guessing you will..."

"I will let you know. What do you think I am a monster?"

Made in the USA
Middletown, DE
25 January 2023

21862840R00031